First Printing: January 2002
Printed in Canada

9 8 7 6 5 4 3 2 1

Penny-Farthing Press, Inc.
10370 Richmond Avenue, Suite 980
Houston, TX 77042
1-800-926-2669

Visit our Web site at www.pfpress.com

Teachers and educators:
If you would like to get more information about Mythics: The Loch series,
coordinating lesson plans, or other available material for educational purposes,
contact Penny-Farthing Press, toll free, at 1-800-926-2669 or go to our Web
site at http://www.pfpress.com/lochlessons/

Library of Congress Cataloging-in-Publishing Data
Maddux, Marlaine.
The Loch, Part III: Discovery
p. cm.
Includes glossary.
ISBN 0-9673683-5-9
1. Maddux, Marlaine.
2001098823

PART III, DISCOVERY

Created and Written by
Marlaine Maddux

Illustrated by
Courtney Huddleston

Inked and Embellished by
Johnny Beware

Colored by
Chris Chuckry

Penny-Farthing Press, Inc. • Houston, Texas

For Harrison;
my grandson and beloved companion
on trips to the land of stories.

~Also~

For Trainor, Valerie, Elaine, and Jim;
because they all understand the importance of adventures.

~And~

For Ken;
because he likes all my stories.

PART III, DISCOVERY

WHAT HAPPENED
IN BOOKS I AND II OF THE LOCH:

IN PART I: FACING THE FUTURE, THE
COUNCIL OF AGES DECIDED THAT OUR
FOUR YOUNG CHARACTERS MUST GO ON A
KNOWLEDGE JOURNEY AROUND THE WORLD
TO BRING BACK INFORMATION ABOUT THE
DRYWALKERS (HUMANS) AND THEIR
ACTIVITIES. THE LOCH MUST ALWAYS BE
ALERT TO POSSIBLE THREATS FROM THESE
CURIOUS AND AGGRESSIVE CREATURES.
AFTER MAKING CAREFUL PREPARATIONS
TO LEAVE THE SAFETY OF THE LOCH,
NESSANDRA, KRAKEY, BOLT, AND ALLURA
IMMEDIATELY FACED THE FIRST CHALLENGE
OF THEIR JOURNEY: THE DANGEROUS
NEPTUNE TUNNEL.

IN PART II: THE KNOWLEDGE JOURNEY,
THEY TRAVEL FROM ONE ADVENTURE TO
ANOTHER IN A QUEST TO LEARN AND TEST
THEMSELVES. FROM LESSONS TAUGHT BY AN
ANCIENT COELACANTH, OLD MON LOUIE,
TO AN ENCOUNTER WITH THE RARE
CADBOROSAURUS, KNOWN AS A "TELLER OF
MAGICAL HISTORY," OUR TRAVELERS MUST
DEVELOP THEIR SKILLS AND EXPAND THEIR
THINKING IN ORDER TO SURVIVE, AND
ULTIMATELY, GROW UP. WITH EVERYTHING
THEY HAVE EXPERIENCED UP TO NOW,
NOTHING COULD HAVE PREPARED THEM
FOR THE EXCITING DISCOVERIES THAT
ARE ABOUT TO TAKE PLACE.

WELCOME TO PART III OF THE LOCH!

THE MAGICAL CITY

Not having much to go on in their search for the magical city of Emperia, our fearless foursome have headed north toward the Bering Strait and on into the Arctic region. Mrs. Cadborosaurus told them everything she knew about finding the mysterious Emperians, but it was not particularly helpful.

First, they must locate the shallow shelf of the Alpha Cordillera Ridge where it rises out of the Lincoln Sea. Then, they are to watch for patches of bright flowers that resemble Blue Bristle and Feather Star. Because there is very little vegetation on the Arctic ocean floor, the flowers should not be difficult to spot. When they notice the flower patches becoming thicker, they are to look for the eight stone peaks that are each topped by a large colored crystal. Standing quietly in the circle formed by the stone peaks, they are to wait for the magical sunbeam to penetrate the water and radiate all eight crystals with a different colored glow. Then, if they are lucky, the majestic gate to the city may become visible and open...or it may not.

THE CIRCLE OF CRYSTALS

"Wow! The crystals are glowing and vibrating!" Bolt says excitedly as everyone turns to look at Allura.

"This feels very familiar," she whispers.

"The crystals are pretty, Allura, but where's the city?" Bolt asks impatiently.

"Shhh..." Nessandra shushes him.

"Oh my goodness...look!" Krakey suddenly shouts.

GASP!

"EMPERIA CITY??"

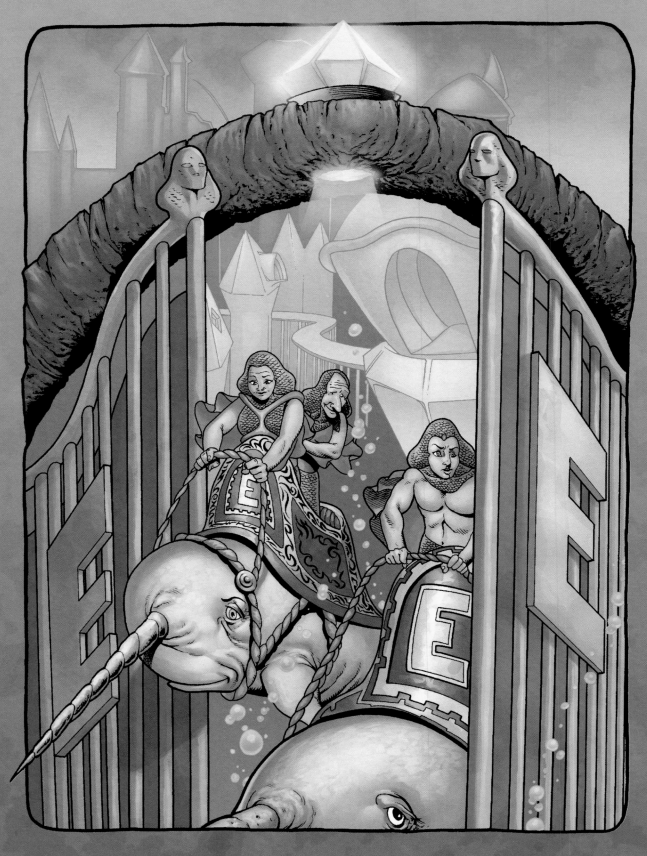

"WHO IS SEEKING ENTRY TO OUR CITY?" shout the Emperian guards as they ride their Narwhal Whales toward our group.

"Oh my, can it be our long lost Princess?" asks the amazed female Emperian. "Is it you, Allura?"

"Yes, Ma'am, it's me. I'm Allura.... Did you say Princess?"

"Yes, yes, the Exalted Empress will be overjoyed," says the friendly potbellied Emperian in front. "She has always prayed for your safe return."

"My name is Surion." The handsome young guard moves forward. "Come, ride with me."

Overwhelmed with excitement, Allura climbs up behind Surion and starts to ride away on the back of the huge Narwhal Whale.

"ON TO THE PALACE!" shout the Emperians.

"You're trembling." Surion turns his head. "I know you must be excited to see your family again."

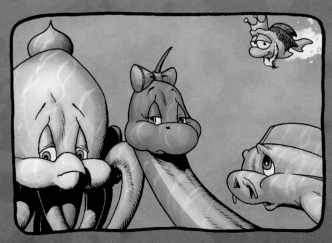

"Where are they going, Nessandra?" Bolt asks in a small voice.

"Wait!" Allura shouts. "My friends! They must come too!"

THE ROYAL THRONE ROOM

The Exalted Empress rises slowly as the strangers enter the throne room.
"Allura?"

"Baby? Is that you?"

"MOTHER?"

"HOORAY!" the overjoyed Emperians cheer as the mother and daughter reunite in a warm embrace.

4

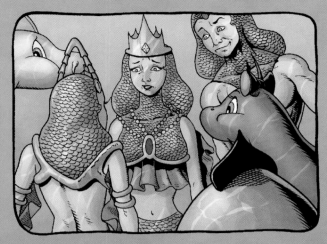 

The Empress can hardly believe her eyes. "After your kidnapping, I feared I would never see you again."

"I was kidnapped?" Allura asks. "Please tell me what happened." Her voice cracks with emotion. "I've lived with dim memories for a long time."

"Oh, Allura, my love, of course you shall hear the story," the Empress promises. "It has been told among the Emperians for many years. Your kidnapping has been one of the saddest chapters in our history."

"No one realized you had slipped outside the gate to play. And you were far too young to know how to easily change dimensions and disappear."

"So you were helpless when the Pinniped walruses swooped down and captured you for trade. They knew you would be a priceless treasure to the drywalkers and that, in exchange, they could receive an endless supply of clams to fill their fat bellies."

"We were soon aware of what had happened, and we formed invisible Emperian search squads who determined that the search direction would be south and east. Our Narwhals contacted the White Beaked Dolphin Patrol in Baffin Bay, and we were told that the kidnapping Pinnipeds had come that way."

"Two of our squads chased the mercenary Pinnipeds around the southern tip of the Baffin Bay Eastern Continent and into Mer Madre. When they caught up with them, you were nowhere to be found."

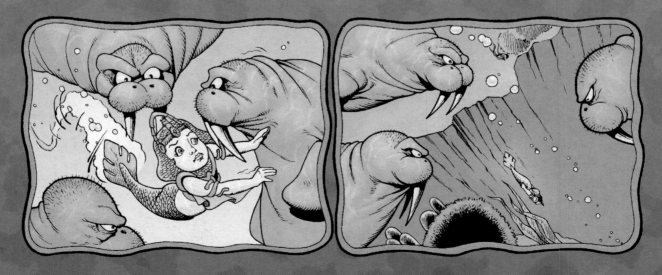

"They claimed you struggled with them..."

"...and swam too deep for them to follow."

"No one could imagine what had happened to you. For many years, our invisible Emperian scouts traveled the world's oceans looking for you, but they never found a trace."

"And now you've come back to us, my beautiful daughter." The Empress smiles. "It's a miracle that you were able to find the city again, and that the gate opened to let you return to our world."

The Empress turns to the others. "You've blessed my daughter with your friendship. You are honored guests in Emperia for as long as you would like to stay."

"Thank you, Ma'am," Nessandra says politely.

"Oh boy!" Krakey grins.

"WOW!" shouts Bolt.

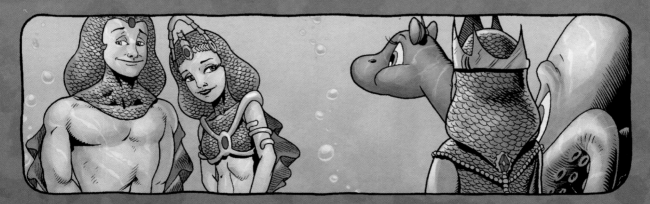

"Now, Allura, it's time for you to reunite with the rest of your fam...oh...." The Empress pauses. "Hmmm...I see you've met Surion."

A FEW WEEKS LATER

"I hope you all understand why I've chosen to stay," Allura says softly.

"Yeah, but I'm going to miss you," Krakey says sadly. "It'll be different. There was nobody else like you in the Loch. "

"Why, Bolt, I didn't know you cared." Allura smiles.

"Ah, Allura, it just won't feel right to go on without you." Bolt looks away.

"I'll always remember the Loch with warm affection, especially you, Bolt. You're becoming a Zeotar who everyone will be proud of." She pauses. "I felt safe and accepted in the Loch, but that didn't stop the deep yearning I had for the place where I knew I belonged."

"Don't be sad. This isn't really goodbye," Allura reassures them. "I'll come visit the Loch again. Besides, look what great adventures you have ahead of you on the rest of the Knowledge Journey.... And," she says excitedly, "the White Beaked Dolphin Patrol has agreed to escort you through Baffin Bay. You couldn't be in better hands. They're powerful and fast swimmers who know their way around the northern seas."

"Things change, Krakey," Allura says gently. "Look at you. You've already changed. You've not only gotten bigger on this trip, you've gotten braver and more grown up. You're not the same person who left the Loch."

"Nessandra, you see, don't you?" Allura pleads. "It isn't only my past I've found in Emperia, the most important thing I've found is my future."

"Yes, I understand, Allura...and I really am happy for you." Nessandra gazes down. "I guess I'm just feeling a little sorry for myself. I'll never be able to have a real future. I mean, I'm the last Plesiosaur, so I'll never have my own family or be able to pass on the thousands of years of Plesiosaur knowledge to my children."

"Bye, Allura."
Nessandra looks back.

"Be happy."

Champ

Though the White Beaked Dolphins were polite and helpful, our travelers were not in the mood to chat. Each one seemed to be adjusting in their own way to the thought of leaving without Allura. Finally, the silence was broken when Nessandra asked one of the Dolphins if they had ever heard of a deep water tunnel that opened on the west side of Mer Madre and emptied into an inland lake in the Western Continent. Gran Mama's journals had mentioned hearing stories of such a tunnel, remarkably similar to the Neptune Tunnel, that was located directly across Mer Madre. Although she never actually found the tunnel herself, Gran Mama always wondered if the rumors were true. When the Dolphin said he HAD heard of such a tunnel, all ears perked up.

"So this is it? Do you know where it goes?" asks Nessandra.

"I'm not sure, but I've heard it empties into a lake far in the interior of the continent," answers the Dolphin.

"Have any White Beaks been there?" she inquires.

"Not in recent times. These waters are close to the Gulf of St. Lawrence and many of the White Beaks have become ill traveling there."

"Why?" asks Krakey.

"The drywalkers have poisoned the water," the Dolphin replies.

"Why?" Krakey asks again.

"We don't know, but until the water is cleaned, our patrols advise White Beaks to avoid it."

"So you know nothing about the tunnel?" Nessandra persists.

"Only that there's a childhood bedtime story among the White Beaks about the three hundred-million-year-old monsters that live in the lake," he says matter-of-factly.

"WHAT?!" Bolt exclaims.

"Oh don't worry, it's only a story...but the White Beaks do avoid this tunnel." He starts to swim away. "Now I have to rejoin the Patrol. Good luck on your journey!"

Krakey looks worried. "What should we do, Nessandra?"

"You tell us, Krakey. What do YOU think we should do?" she asks.

"I think we should go! I mean, WOW! Just imagine what we might find!"

"Bolt, let Krakey decide," Nessandra says firmly.

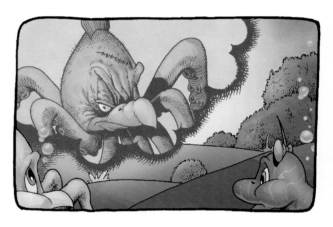 

"Well, we don't have any idea what might be there." Krakey hesitates as he imagines the possibilities.

"Right," she answers.

"But we're supposed to be exploring for knowledge," he says.

"Right," she agrees.

"And the Loch expects us to bring back new information." Krakey's voice is growing stronger.

"Right," Nessandra repeats. "Then should we go?"

"YES, let's go!" shouts a determined Krakey.

"Hooray!" Bolt exclaims, dashing ahead.

DEEP INSIDE THE TUNNEL

"Nessandra, look!" Bolt calls. "Those are light crystals just like we use in the Loch."

"Where did those come from?" she asks with surprise. "This is getting more and more interesting."

"Krakey, how are you doing?" Nessandra checks on her friend.

"Fine, I guess. HEY! Look at that opening!" he shouts. "We must be coming into the lake."

"WOW! Who are you?!" Bolt hurries toward the strangers.

"Well, really! Do you get that kind of response when others meet YOU for the first time?" one creature asks in disgust. "You're rather strange looking too, you know."

"I didn't mean it that way. I've just never met anyone like you," Bolt apologizes.

"Well, you're obviously not familiar with the Tully Monster...even though we've been around for three-hundred-million years," he says smugly.

"So you're the monsters!" Krakey laughs with relief.

"How rude! What are you laughing at, young man?!" The Tully Monster is indignant.

"I'm sorry. We thought you were vicious monsters...I mean...you know," Nessandra tries to explain. "Give us another chance to introduce ourselves. We're guests in your lake and I'm afraid we're behaving badly."

"Don't mind them," a booming voice declares. "They're overly sensitive... especially since we can all see right through them."

"A Plesiosaur?" Nessandra gasps.

"Who asked you, Champ?" one of the Tully Monsters responds to the newcomer. "This lack of respect goes way back. Even our ancient ancestors from the middle regions complained of it."

"So I guess your sensitive nature must be genetic," Champ jokes.

"Oh be quiet, Champ!" the Tully Monster complains. "Just because we're transparent, doesn't mean you can talk about us like we're not here."

"Sorry, Tully, just kidding." Champ smiles.

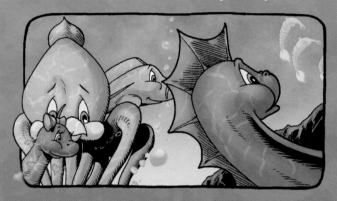

"But they really are overly sensitive," Champ whispers as he turns his attention to our four. "You've come through the tunnel. So where might you be..."

"...from?" He suddenly notices Nessandra.

"We're from the Loch," Bolt answers. "We're on a Knowledge Journey, so we thought we had better...."

"Bolt, I don't think they're listening," Krakey laughs. "Maybe we should explore on our own for a while."

"Oh yeah, I see what you mean. Let's go."

"I'm Nessandra. Did I hear the Tully Monsters call you Champ?" Nessandra gazes up at the handsome Plesiosaur.

"Yeah, my dad named me after the lake."

"This is Lake Champ?" Nessandra asks innocently.

"Not exactly," Champ chuckles, and notices Nessandra is embarrassed.

"I'm sorry, I didn't mean to laugh," he apologizes. "It's just obvious that you've never been here before."

"No, I'm from the Loch, on the other side of Mer Madre," she explains. "We were exploring your lake as part of our Knowledge Journey."

"Your what?"

"Well, you see, in the Loch..." Nessandra begins her story.

A LITTLE LATER

"Now that you've heard all about us, tell me about you...and the lake...and your parents," Nessandra requests.

"Okay, but one thing at a time," Champ answers. "My mother died when I was born and my father raised me."

"What about brothers and sisters, or aunts and uncles?" she persists.

"Nope. My dad and I were the last of our species," he says regretfully.

"What do you mean...were?"

"My dad died about a year ago...now I'm the last one," he says quietly.

"So you live here alone?"

"Yep, just me and the Tully Monsters and all the other fish in the lake." Champ tries to sound cheerful, but sadness fills his eyes.

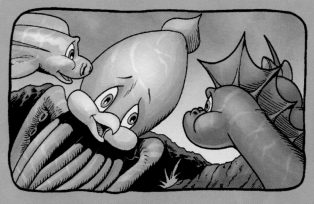 

"Nessandra, Nessandra!" Bolt shouts. "There's a strange humming sound in the water over there."

"Oh, don't worry," Champ reassures, "that's only my signal."

"What signal?" asks a puzzled Nessandra.

"The one my friend Wyatt Jordan uses when he wants to speak with me," Champ explains.

"WHAT!!" They're all shocked by the news.

"Oh sure. He signals me and I surface in Mallet's Bay to see what he wants."

"You surface?!" they ask in unison.

"Not often, but I do for Wyatt Jordan. I haven't seen him since my father died," he says expectantly. "Come on, you can go with me to meet him."

"Oh no!" refuses Nessandra. "Surfacing in the Loch is a sacred honor for the Ness, and only for the ones who've been through the Rite of Arcking."

"Oh. Well, wait for me here then. I'll be back soon. Okay?" Champ asks as he hurries off toward Mallet's Bay.

MALLET'S BAY

"Champ, old man, how are you? And how's your father feeling?"
Wyatt Jordan greets his friend.

"My dad died last year," Champ says sadly.

"Oh...I'm sorry. The last time I spoke with him, he feared the sickness had gone too far," the drywalker says sympathetically.

"Before he died, he warned me that if I ever left the tunnel, I was not to swim in the gulf waters north of here. He was convinced THAT was what made him sick."

"I know, that's why I wanted to see you. The International Council of Ocean Regulation has agreed to hear my report on how we can clean up and preserve our seas,"
Jordan says hopefully.

"Good! Maybe they'll listen this time," Champ encourages. "By the way, have you discovered any more strange creatures in your travels?"

"As a matter of fact, I recently helped rescue a Cadborosaurus from capture by some scientists. I also was completely surprised when I saw a prehistoric creature that reminded me of you," Wyatt Jordan says enthusiastically.

"Oh really? Well, I just might have something here in my lake that would interest you," Champ teases.

"Really? What?"

"You'll have to wait and see." Champ starts to sink below the surface.
"Good luck with the Council."

CHAMP AND NESSANDRA

TWO WEEKS LATER

"You've never been out of the tunnel?"
Nessandra asks.

"Nope. My dad thought it was too dangerous.
He rarely went out himself," Champ answers.

"How did you get the crystals that light the tunnel?"

"My mom brought those back from Atlantis
before I was born."

"How will you replace them?" She sounds concerned.

"It doesn't matter." Champ's eyes look sad. "I won't be using the tunnel."

"NESSAAANDRAAA!"
Bolt calls in a loud voice. "When are we leaving? Krakey and I have explored every corner of the lake twice."

"I know, I know...we'll leave tomorrow. Go say goodbye to the Tully Monsters. I'll join you later," she says impatiently.

She softens her voice, though, and asks Champ an important question. "Champ, would you ever think about coming back to the Loch with us?"

YIPPEE!

"I thought you'd never ask!" Champ jumps for joy.

"But wait," he says. "Are you asking because you feel sorry for me?"

"No, no, I don't feel sorry for you...I mean... I'm sorry you're alone," she stammers.

"You love me, don't you, Nessandra?" Champ insists. "Krakey told me about the Tulip Tail."

"Yes, you're right." She looks embarrassed.

"Well, I love you too, Nessandra," he says boldly, "and I want you to be my WIFE!"

Krakey and Bolt stare in amazement. "Bolt, do you think Nessandra's changed?" Krakey asks as his cheeks turn red.

Nessandra suddenly hears Gran Ness's voice and is startled by the Link. "Mother? Is that you?"

"Hello, my darling. I'm confident you're well and safe," Gran Ness says as she Links with Nessandra. "I would know if you were in trouble."

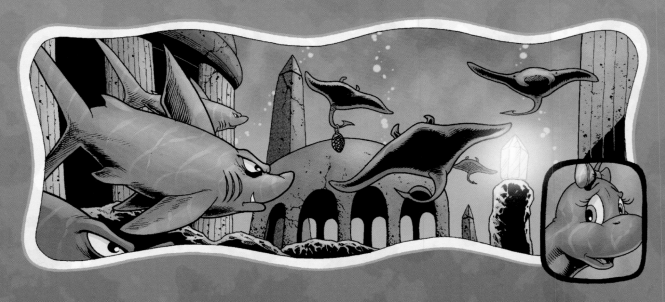

"I'm Linking to give you vital information about your visit to Atlantis," Gran Ness continues. "Renegade Thresher Sharks are waging guerilla warfare against the Atlantean crystal traders to get control of the profitable crystal trade. Be alert and be careful."

"I'll be careful, Mother...and...by the way...have I got news for you!"

3

CRYSTALS OF LIGHT

There is a reason the final stop on the Knowledge Journey is Atlantis and the crystal trade. Not only are the crystals too valuable to transport, but the extra time gives our journeyers an opportunity to create their critical limerick. The crystal traders are legendary collectors of original limericks, and they are the only articles of trade they will accept in exchange for the precious crystals. While Nessandra is in a particularly joyous mood with the exuberant Champ at her side, she is still worried about the unsettling news sent through the telepathic Link by her mother. Negotiating with the crystal traders is stressful enough without having to face bands of renegade raiders.

"Look at this whole wide ocean," Champ declares. "It's beautiful!"

"You haven't seen anything yet," Nessandra laughs.

"What d'ya think, Krakey?" Bolt whispers. "Is he a little nuts?"

"This old map isn't much help." Nessandra furrows her brow as she examines the document. "But I think we should go east to the Azores Plateau."

"We'll probably find markers there we can follow...I hope," she murmurs.

"Lead the way, Nessandra," Champ says cheerfully. "You know I'll follow you anywhere."

"Oh, brother." Bolt rolls his eyes.

THE AZORES PLATEAU

"I wonder where we go from here?" Nessandra says. "I can see we're in the area, but where's Lyrian City?"

"Why don't we ask those fish over there?" Champ suggests.

"You mean that school of Barracudas?" Krakey asks. "Not a chance. They're too stuck-up to speak to us."

"Yes, but they do seem to know where they're going," Nessandra observes.

"I'll ask for directions!" Bolt volunteers.

"Hey, we're a little lost and we need some help," Bolt says as he approaches the Barracudas.

"Are you speaking to us? Don't you know we don't talk to strangers? We're Snooty Barracudas." They look at Bolt like he's crazy.

"So what?" Bolt continues to ignore their rudeness. "We only want to ask you how to get to Lyrian City."

"You actually want to talk with us?" asks the first Barracuda in disbelief.

"With us?" a second Barracuda asks.

"Well, what a relief!" the third Barracuda says. "No one has wanted to talk with us for ages. You can't imagine how tiring it is to be snooty!"

"Where are you from?"

"What are your names?"

"Why are you here?"

"Where are you going?"

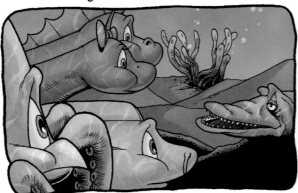

Then, just as suddenly, the Barracudas stop and take a deep breath. "My, that was refreshing conversation. Let's do it again.... Oh! And if you want to find Lyrian City, follow the Mid Madre Ridge south to the edge of the Sargasso Sea," the first Barracuda says in a rush. "The Blue Manta guards will meet you there and guide you the rest of the way."

"But..." stammers Champ.

"TA-TA for now!" The second Barracuda turns back. "Great conversation!"

"Huh?" our four murmur.

SOME TIME LATER

"This is definitely an Atlantean village outpost, but where are the Blue Mantas?" Nessandra asks.

"Things don't look right here," Champ observes.

"Nessandra, look over there!" Bolt shouts. "Something's glowing."

Nessandra spots the two Blue Mantas near the glowing crystal and signals the others to follow her in that direction.

The entire village had been destroyed except for two Manta guardians and a lone crystal.

"What's happened here? Where is everyone?" Nessandra asks.

"Some are dead," answers the hovering Manta. "The rest have gone to Lyrian City. It's safer there."

"Safer from what?" Champ asks.

"The Thresher Sharks invaded our village," the standing Manta answers. "They found all the crystals except the healing prism. It is one of the most valuable crystals and we must not let it fall into their hands."

"You mean that one?"
Nessandra asks.

"Yes, we're healing our wounds."

"Are you badly hurt?" Nessandra
is concerned.

"A few more minutes with the
prism and we'll be fine," he assures
her. "Are you in Atlantis to trade
for crystals?"

"Yes, but we need directions
to Lyrian City."

"One of us can guide you,"
the hovering Manta offers, "but
the other must stay and guard this
crystal. The Threshers may realize
they've missed it."

"Why are the Threshers doing this?"
Champ asks.

"Whoever controls the crystals
has great power," the standing
Manta answers.

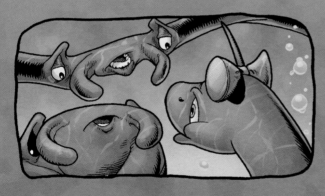

"Haven't there been other outsiders
who've attempted to steal the
crystals?" Nessandra asks.

"Yes, but the Shimmering Solons
have always shown them the folly
of such actions," he answers.

"Are the Shimmering Solons
the leaders of Atlantis?"
Nessandra inquires.

"They are the 'wise ones' and can
usually reason with outsiders,"
the Manta explains.

"The Threshers, however, are
aggressive and growing in number.
They don't see the danger of putting
these crystals in the wrong hands,"
says the other Manta.

"Uh oh, listen. Hear the clicking?
The Sharks are returning!"

"CIRCLE THE CRYSTAL!"
the Mantas shout.

"We'll help you!" Nessandra yells.

"GET READY!" instruct the Mantas. "They're attacking!"

The Threshers quickly recognize the strangers' superior fighting abilities.

"EEEOOWW!" the Sharks yell when they discover they do not hold the upper hand.

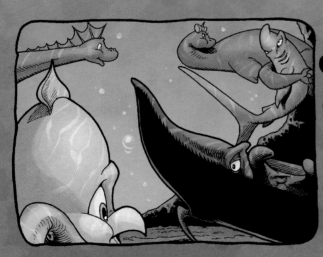 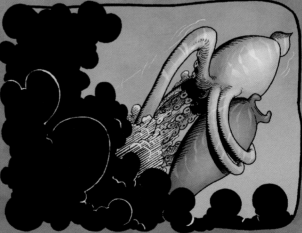

"Nice pin, Nessandra!" Champ laughs as Krakey notices one of the Mantas is in trouble.

"You're wounded," he says.

"If I could get inside a building, I'll be okay. But they'll see me and attack," he says weakly.

"Leave it to me," Krakey promises. "I'll hide you in my ink!"

"OOPS, sorry about the headache!" Champ chuckles.

"BACK OFF, THRESHER!" Nessandra yells angrily as she tosses him over her shoulder.

"Two Sharks with one charge! Who says we're outnumbered?!" Bolt cries triumphantly.

"Don't take this as a HUG!" Krakey says as he rejoins the battle.

"WAIT, ZEOTAR! Forget them!" the Manta shouts. "Let them report to their leaders that fighting us for the crystals won't be so easy!"

After the Threshers retreat, the Manta turns to his new friends. "You are worthy fighters. Thank you for defending our crystal. Come, let me take you to Lyrian City."

LYRIAN CITY

"Here it is...Lyrian City!" the Blue Manta proudly announces. "We sent word for them to expect you, and we informed the Shimmering Solons of your defense of the healing crystal."

"Where do we go to offer our limerick?" Nessandra asks.

"The Sanctuary Room is in the great pyramid down there. I will escort you," he answers.

"We enter here." The Blue Manta shows the way through an open door.

Nessandra is amazed by the long line. "Are all of them here to trade for crystals?"

"Yes, they're waiting to see one of the Shimmering Solons," he answers. "The Solons are the limerick listeners."

THE IMPORTANT MOMENT

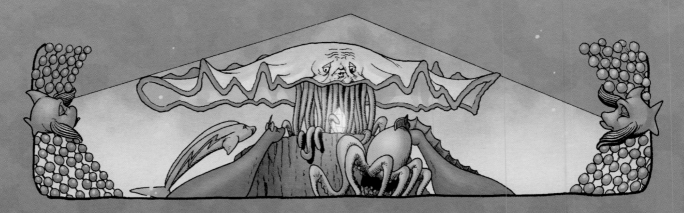

"I hope your wait was not long." The Shimmering Solon speaks in a strong, clear voice. "I understand you are here to earn new crystals for the Loch."

"Yes, sir," Nessandra says nervously.

"Very well," he continues, "do you have any questions before I listen to your limerick?"

"I do, sir," Champ speaks up. "Why do you trade crystals for limericks? Why not ask for gold and jewels?"

"Gold and jewels are not valuable to us. We want to improve our undersea world through the use of the crystals."

"But what do limericks have to do with that?" Bolt jumps in.

"It teaches those who wish to use the crystals how to be smarter and how to appreciate their true value.

"HUH?" Krakey looks confused.

"Creating a limerick will often help them identify the problems that brought them to us in the first place...and sometimes even how to solve those problems," he patiently explains. "We want to trade our crystals to communities of thinkers. Now may I hear your limerick?"

"Yes, sir...here goes."
Nessandra gulps as she notices his stern expression.

"We need the new crystals for light.
Without them, our world isn't bright.
If you think this a jest,
And deny our request,
We will live in perpetual night!"

"Hmmm...yes, well you've told me what the crystals can do for you," he ponders, "but have you really shown them proper respect? I think you should try again."

"Oh, no! What will we do?" they panic. "We can't go back to the Loch without the crystals!"

"Can you Link with Gran Ness?" Krakey asks.

"No, Krakey, the Council of Ages trusted US with this mission," Nessandra says calmly. "The four of us can do this. We've been under pressure before. It might have taken us a long time to write our first limerick, but we are smarter now and can think faster....
Let's concentrate!"

They huddle together....

"Okay, sir, we're ready to recite our new limerick," Nessandra says as they all move forward.

"Yes," the Shimmering Solon nods, "go ahead."

Nessandra takes a deep breath.

"The crystals are precious, we know.
We value the light that they throw.
Unlike the shark,
Who favors the dark,
The Loch will give thanks for the glow."

"Hmmm...." The Solon's face is serious as he ponders their limerick.

"Yes...yes...well done!" He finally smiles. "You've shown deeper appreciation for a treasure that brings light and healing to our undersea world." He pauses. "Your crystals may be collected in the next chamber. Do you have any questions?"

"I do, I do!" Bolt exclaims. "What are you going to do about the Thresher Sharks?"

"You are the Zeotar," the Solon acknowledges. "We have received reports of your brave defense of our crystal. I will answer your question."

"Attacks from the outside have been a recurring event in our long history," he tells them. "They never succeed."

"Why?" Bolt asks.

"Because only we, the traders and guardians of the crystals, know how to control the power of this energy," the Solon continues.

"If negotiations fail and we are forced to use this power against the Threshers, we will."

"Ooooh..." our group responds knowingly.

"Now it is time for you to pick up your crystals and return home to the Loch. Good luck and safe passage on your journey."

Back to the Loch

heading for home! Can it be that the Knowledge Journey is almost over? Spirits are high, except for Champ's nervousness about meeting Nessandra's parents. But nothing can spoil the group's mood...not even meeting cranky residents of the Mid Madre Ridge. Yes, as far as they're concerned, it's all smooth sailing as they approach the challenging waters of the Neptune Tunnel and the final leg of their journey home. They are all anticipating the glorious warm welcome they will receive at the Loch. But...as they soon discover, it will be a much different story.

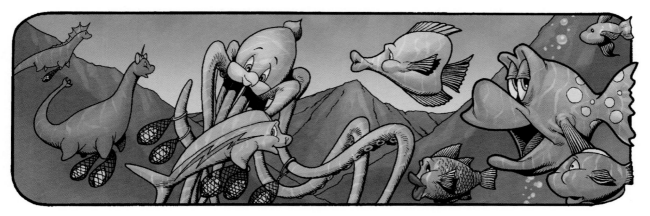

"Are you sure you know how to find the Neptune Tunnel, Nessandra?"
Bolt asks.

"I'm sure," she answers. "One thing the Loch maps are very clear
about is how to return to the tunnel."

"Look everyone, isn't that the Mid Madre Ridge?" Krakey points out.

"Good job, Krakey!" Nessandra compliments. "We're supposed to follow
it north to the Neptune Tunnel mountain range."

"Why is Champ lagging so far
behind?" Nessandra looks back.

"What's wrong, Champ.
Are you sick?"

"No, I was thinking about the
Loch...and your mom and dad. Do
you think they'll like me?" he asks.

"Champ, they're going to like you more than you can possibly imagine," she reassures him.

"I hope so," Champ says.

"Are those two acting googly-eyed again?" Bolt turns to look at them.

"Bolt!" Nessandra yells. "You dropped a crystal!"

"Oh gosh! I'll get it!" He watches it fall and swoops down after it.

"OUCH! Who bonked me on the head? I can't even stick my head out to see what kind of DAY it is," says a very cranky Wolf Eel, emerging from his home.

"Gee, I'm sorry, the crystal slipped," Bolt apologizes.

Mrs. Eel pops her head out.
"Is it a sniggler?!"

"No, no. It's only a pest,"
Mr. Eel rudely replies.

"Gee, I'm sorry," Bolt apologizes
again. "It was an accident."

"Go away! We're cranky,
leave us alone."

Mr. and Mrs. Eel's seven children suddenly join the conversation.

"I'm hungry!"

"It's too crowded in here!"

"I can't sleep!"

"I want to go outside!"

"BE QUIET!" Mr. Eel yells at them.

"Oops, looks like your whole family's cranky," Bolt laughs.
"I'll just pick up the crystal and be on my way."

"Yes, yes, leave us alone! We're cranky! We're cranky!" Mr. Eel shouts.

NEARING HOME

"There it is!" Bolt says excitedly.
"The Neptune Tunnel!"

"What is that?" They look
in amazement.

"My, oh my. Who is this motley crew?" Horgum reveals his ugly head.
"And what treasures are you carrying there?"

"Out of the way, Horgum!" Nessandra orders. "We have to catch the inland
current that carries us to the Loch."

"Well...hasn't the little girl grown
into a tough talker?" Horgum
speaks in his sweet and oily voice.

"You're right, I have." Nessandra
stands up to him. "Maybe I was
afraid of you once, but now I've seen
things a whole lot scarier than you!"

Champ pushes forward.
"Move aside, Nessandra.
Let me handle this."

"Who do we have here? Your HERO?"
Horgum laughs sarcastically.

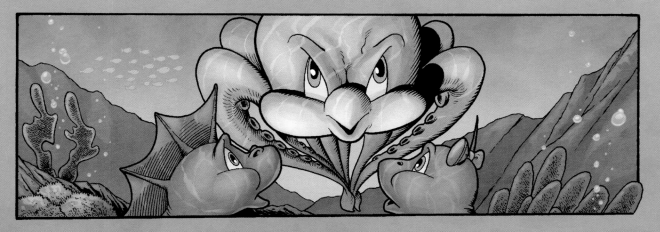

Krakey suddenly swoops over their heads. "Move back, you two. This is MY job!"

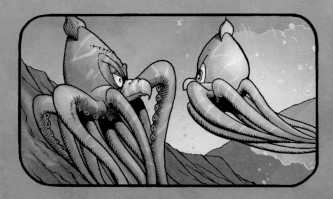

"If you're looking for trouble, Horgum, then deal with ME!"

"ANYTIME YOU'RE READY!" Krakey challenges.

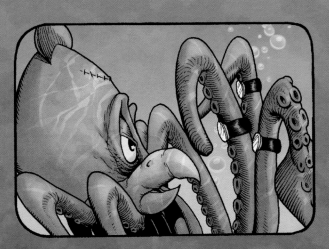

"My, my." Horgum backs away. "Did I say I had time to chat? I was mistaken. I see that I'm late for a dinner appointment. TA-TA for now."

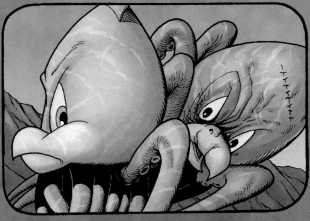

Horgum swims away, but growls as he passes Krakey. "Next time...KRAKEN!"

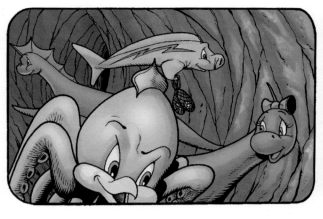

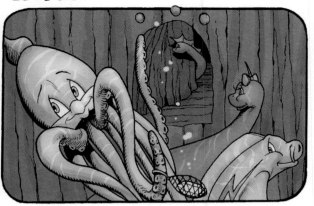

"Wow, Krakey! That was impressive! He called you KRAKEN!" Nessandra says with admiration.

"Yeah, I heard." Krakey grins shyly.

"We're making good time," Nessandra observes. "We're already in Nineteen Door Bay." She looks back at the three circles over the door...and the reluctant Champ. "Champ, are you coming?"

"Are you still worried?" She smiles. "I've told you that my parents will like you."

"I'm not so sure, Nessandra. You ARE their only daughter." Champ looks unconvinced.

"Trust me, Champ." She continues to smile knowingly.

As they swim past Morag's portal, a friendly voice calls out.

"The travelers are home, my greetings they spurn. The Loch cannot wait for your speedy return?"

Nessandra answers:
"Sorry, Morag, we don't mean to rush by. At some other time, we would stop and say hi."

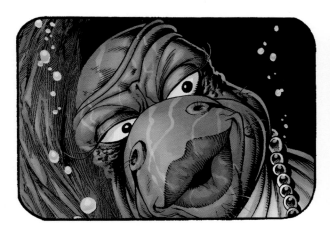

"And who is this chap,
Anyone I know?
By the look on your face,
Could it be a new beau?"

"You guessed it, Morag,
He's joining my life.
Champ is his name,
And I'll soon be his wife."

ALMOST THERE

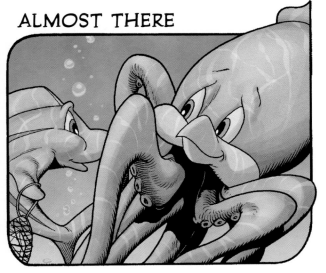

"Gee, she was odd," observes Champ.

"Get ready to meet LOTS
of interesting characters,"
Nessandra jokes.

"The Loch portal is just ahead,"
says Bolt excitedly. "Get ready
to catch on, Krakey."

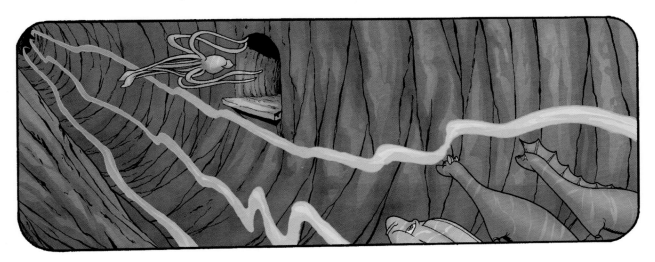

"The current is strong," Nessandra warns Champ. "It's easier for Krakey
because he has so many arms to grab with."

"C'mon, Bolt, I did it,
you can make it!" yells Krakey.

"Pull, Nessandra, PULL!"
Bolt and Krakey cheer.

"OOPS," says Krakey as he grabs
Champ's tail. "You've gone too far!"

"Thanks, Krakey." Champ blushes.

"You'll get the hang of it,"
Krakey assures him.

As the explorers emerge from the Neptune Tunnel into the Loch,
they are greeted by an eerie silence.

"Where is everyone?" Nessandra's heart sinks.

"I told you they didn't want to meet me," Champ says dejectedly.

Rituals

Of course, the surprise planned by the citizens of the Loch turned out to be a grand party and hero's welcome. The excitement could be felt throughout the community as everyone anticipated the special rituals to come. First, Nessandra must go through the Rite of Arcking. Then the Passage of Leadership ceremony would take place so Nessandra could step into the role she was born to inherit. As if that was not enough to look forward to, no one had dreamed there would be a Plesiosaur wedding. Gran Ness and Mon Ness must first give their blessings for this event to occur, so everyone is nervously awaiting their decision.

For such a happy time, there was only one sad note... the absence of Allura.

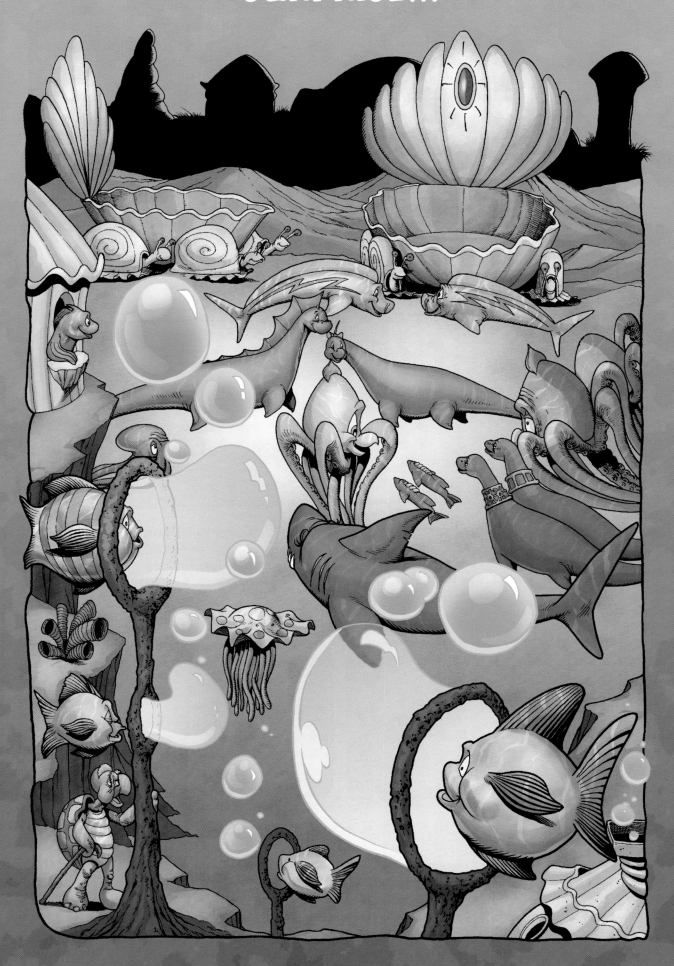

BACK HOME

"That was a wonderful celebration for your homecoming, dear,"
Gran Ness comments.

"Mother, Father, you haven't been
formally introduced to Champ,"
Nessandra speaks up.
"Champ, meet my parents."

"Hello, Champ," Gran Ness says
rather coolly. "Nessandra tells us
you are from a lake in the
Western Continent."

"Well, well...the old stories must
have been true." Mon Ness looks
Champ over carefully. "Other
families like us DO live across
Mer Madre in a faraway lake."
He pauses. "You look like a
strong, young Plesiosaur. Are
your other relatives like you?"

"No, sir, I'm the only one left,"
Champ says shyly. "My father
died last year."

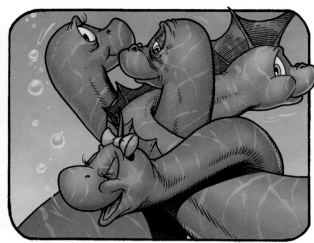

"Oh?" Mon Ness looks at him with kindness. "Nessandra tells us she loves you...and I can see you feel the same."

"Sooo..."

"WELCOME TO OUR FAMILY...SON!"

THE KRAKENS

"Son, the Knowledge Journey has obviously been good for you," Mon Kraken says in his deep voice. "You've grown into a full-sized Kraken and you're almost as tall as I am."

"Yes, sir." Krakey smiles.

"That is a small accomplishment," his mother says lovingly, "compared to the growth of your heart."

"Oh, Mom." Krakey blushes.

BOLT AND MON ZEOTAR

"I've heard the stories of your courage, Bolt," Mon Zeotar says proudly. "I'm not surprised. I knew you were brave. Tell me what other things you learned on the Knowledge Journey."

"I learned that the world was exciting, Dad...and dangerous!"

"What else, Bolt...what else did you learn?" Mon Zeotar presses.

"That my charges had to be straight and strong if they would protect us...and, that I always did better when I followed the group's original plans."

"Good, son, good!" congratulates Mon Zeotar. "You've learned a great lesson among Zeotars. You've learned the power of discipline!"

"Oh...yeah...I guess I have," Bolt realizes.

DAYS LATER

"There's so much to tell you that I hardly know where to begin. First, I'm getting married tomorrow! His name is Champ, Gran Mama, and he's of the same ancestry that we are. You can imagine that Mother and Father are thrilled with the thought of having grandchildren."

"But I mustn't get too far ahead of myself. Tomorrow's ceremony will be unique in the history of the Loch. The Council has decided to combine my wedding with the Rite of Arcking, AND, they have given permission for Champ to arc with me!"

"Gran Mama, before I left the Loch on the Knowledge Journey, Father told me I would learn about myself by meeting others. I didn't know what he meant. Now I do. At each of the places I visited, I tried to picture myself fitting into that world. Along the way, I began to feel sure about where I belonged. I saw those same feelings in Allura when she found Emperia."

"Now, I know that the rituals of the Loch, along with my ancestry and history, are a big part of who I am. Thank you, Gran Mama, for helping me find my way home."

"Nessandra! Nessandra!" Bolt races up. "Guess who came to visit?!"

"Did you think we would miss your wedding and Rite of Arcking?" Allura smiles.

MON LIPILUNG MARRIES THE HAPPY COUPLE

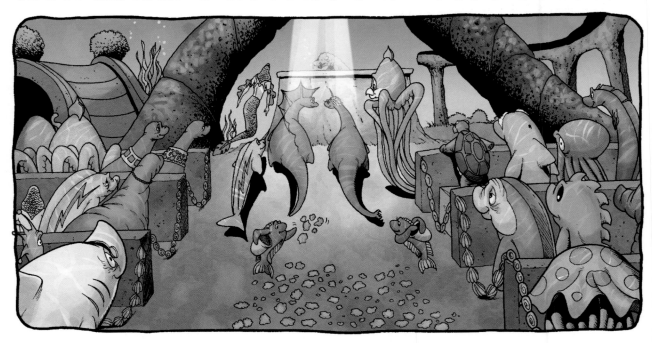

"I now declare you husband and wife. May the Plesiosaur line continue through the ages."

"CONGRATULATIONS!"

"The wedding was lovely, darling," Gran Ness says happily, "and the sacred Rite of Arcking will be a perfect ceremony for you and Champ to bond your vows. Remember, though, arcking can be dangerous. If you see any drywalkers, submerge immediately."

"BONDOLAY!" the crowd cheers as Champ and Nessandra swim higher and higher toward the opening to Loch Ness.

"BONDOLAY!!"

"Champ! Quick, look!" Nessandra urges. "There's a drywalker!
We have to go down!"

"No, wait, Nessandra," laughs Champ,
"that's Wyatt Jordan!"

"What?!" She blinks.

"C'mon, let's go talk to him."
He swims away.

"I dunno...." Nessandra hangs back.

"CHAMP, old man, what are
you doing here?" Wyatt Jordan
looks surprised.

"Meet my wife, Nessandra," Champ
says proudly. "This is my new home."

"What terrific news!" Wyatt Jordan
grins. "Nessandra, it is my pleasure.
But...wait...haven't we met before?
Aren't you the one who protected
the Cadborosaurus half-way around
the world from here?"

"Yes...that was me," she says shyly.

"Bravo! You were splendid," he remembers. "So you're the creature who lives here in Loch Ness?"

"Well, it's a bit more complicated than that, but yes, I live here."

"Wyatt, her Loch...our Loch, is a hidden world and we want to keep it that way," Champ explains.

"You needn't be concerned, Nessandra," Jordan reassures her. "I can tell that the Loch is very special, and I'll always keep your secret. The purpose of my life and work is helping rare creatures. Seeing them survive and flourish in their natural homes makes me happy."

"Old Mon Louie was right. You are our friend." Nessandra smiles. "Even though you're a drywalker."

"Who? What?" he asks.

"Never mind," she chuckles.

"We have to go back now," Champ says. "It's dangerous to be on the surface too long. By the way, what did the ocean regulation group say about your report?"

"They listened." Jordan's voice was hopeful. "Now we'll have to wait and see."

"I'm pleased to have met you, Mr. Jordan," Nessandra says politely. "Perhaps you can visit again."

"You can count on it, Nessandra. And please call me Wyatt. CONGRATULATIONS! I wish you both well," he says softly as he waves goodbye.

CORONATION DAY

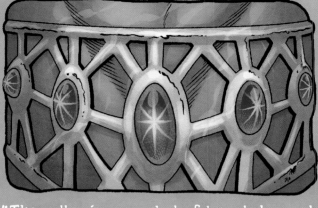

"It's time, Nessandra, for you to inherit the collar," Gran Ness speaks seriously to her daughter. "From today forward, you will lead the Loch into a new era."

"The collar is a symbol of knowledge and history. Citizens of the Loch will look to you for wise decisions. It is not an easy burden to carry," Gran Ness continues.

"An important piece of advice for the new Ness leader of the Loch is to learn to trust your gift of foresight, Nessandra. As you get older, it will become stronger. Listen to it."

"When has it helped YOU, Mother?" Nessandra asks.

"When you left on your Knowledge Journey, I was very afraid," Gran Ness reveals. "But my foresight made me know that this trip was extremely important for you. Not only because of the reasons stated by the Council of Ages, but because I knew the key to your destiny was somewhere outside the Loch. So you see...now we have Champ. Come, it is time to get the festivities under way."

THE GATHERING

"Citizens of the Loch!" Gran Ness announces. "The first phase of today's ceremony will be to present the 'learnings' from Nessandra's Knowledge Journey."

"We have learned that the drywalkers' science is advancing rapidly," Mon Torto reports.

"We have also learned that we have friends among the drywalkers who will fight for our good," Mon Coelacanth says hopefully.

"And, as we often learn from the Knowledge Journeys, all other beings in the deep waters of the world are struggling to keep order and to survive in the face of constant threats," Gran Pucashark adds.

"Finally, for now," Mon Lipilung says as he steps forward, "we've learned the Loch is SAFE!"

"HOORAY!!" the crowd cheers.

The End

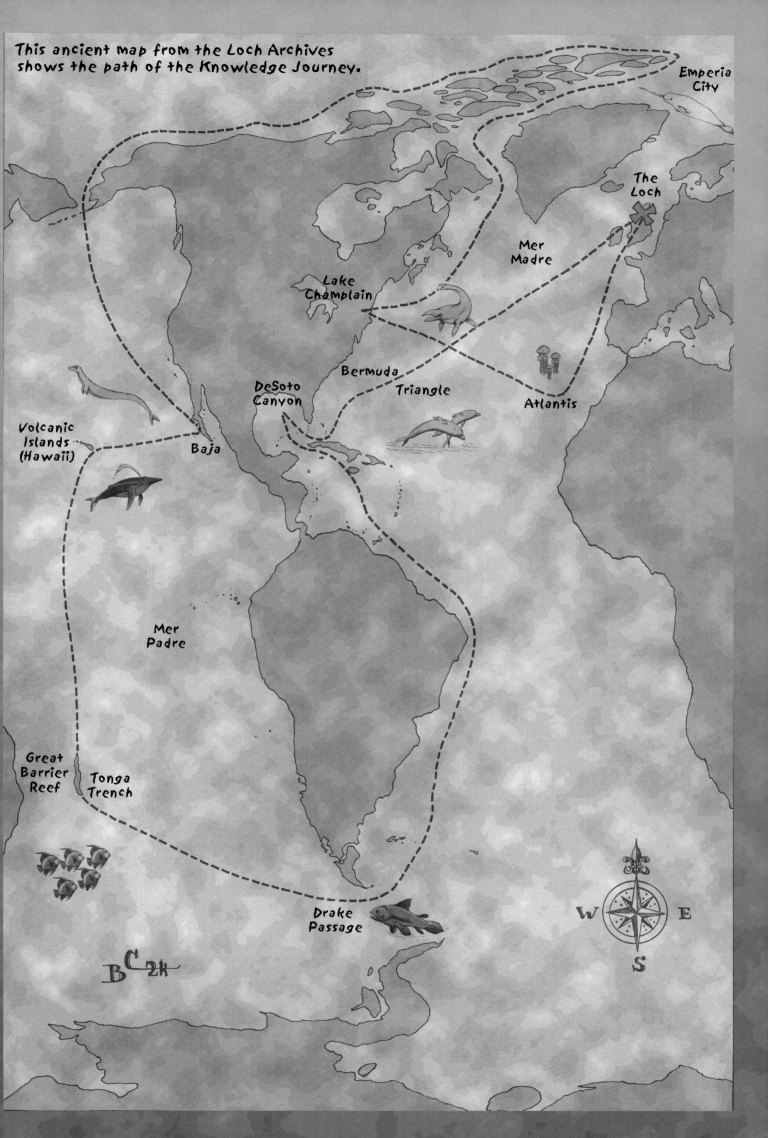

This ancient map from the Loch Archives shows the path of the Knowledge Journey.

Emperia City

The Loch

Mer Madre

Lake Champlain

Bermuda Triangle

DeSoto Canyon

Atlantis

Volcanic Islands (Hawaii)

Baja

Mer Padre

Great Barrier Reef

Tonga Trench

Drake Passage

W E

S

Loch Ness

The Loch

the Loch Lexicon

PART III

A Glossary for Drywalkers

Alpha Cordillera Ridge (al-fa cor-di-lare-uh rige) – Larger in area than the Alps of Switzerland, the Alpha Cordillera Ridge is a rugged ocean mountain chain extending from the southern waters of Iceland to the extreme South Atlantic Ocean. Despite its enormous size, it has remained a relative mystery to the drywalkers who only discovered it in the 1950s. Silly drywalkers! The creatures of the sea have known of it for hundreds of years!

Atlantis – Far from the safety of the Loch, Atlantis is the legendary sunken island where our travelers must bargain for the precious light crystals that keep the Loch inhabitants from the darkness.

Azores Plateau (a-zor-ez pla-tow) – A morphological feature in the Atlantic Ocean caused by volcanic activity. The plateau supports the Azores Islands and is located near the Eurasian and African continental plates.

Baffin Bay – An arm of the North Atlantic Ocean with a harsh climate and a generally hostile environment, Baffin Bay does not seem like the kind of place where wildlife would abound. The severity of the surroundings, however, is exactly what makes it a haven for a wide variety of animal and plant species, both in the ocean and on land, because most drywalkers do not want to venture there.

Barracuda (bear-uh-coo-duh) – The snooty barracuda are members of the family of barracuda known as the Atlantic Barracuda or Great Barracuda. They are not called "great" because they are particularly friendly or nice (in fact, they prefer to be left alone), but because of their enormous size. They can reach from five to eight feet in length!

Bering Strait – Separating Siberia, Russia, and Alaska, USA, the Bering Strait connects the Arctic Ocean to the Bering Sea. Nessandra and her friends travel this route after leaving Mrs. Cadborosaurus in their search to find the Magical City.

Beau (bow) – Another word for boyfriend or sweetheart.

Blue Bristle – A rare underwater plant only found near Emperia City that is bright blue in color with long, spiked bristles.

Blue Manta – Although closely related to sharks, you will never see a manta bearing his teeth at anything because they do not have any! Manta rays are plankton eaters who sieve the ocean waters for microscopic foodstuffs. Despite the size of what they eat, mantas are very powerful and can grow up to 22 feet from wing tip to wing tip!

Chamber – A room or enclosed space. In Lyrian City, the valuable light crystals are kept in a special, guarded chamber.

Citizen – A resident or member of a city, state, or nation.

Council of Ages – Legendary panel made up of the oldest and wisest creatures that live in the Loch. Their knowledge and experience earn them great respect among the Loch inhabitants. They are always consulted in times of crisis and need.

Crystal Traders – See Shimmering Solons.

Decree – An official announcement, order, or decision.

Drywalkers – What the inhabitants of the Loch call humans.

Eastern Continent – What the creatures of the sea call Greenland.

Emperia (em-peer-ee-uh) – The real name of the Magical City, "Emperia" is what its citizens call their home.

Emperians (em-peer-ee-ans) – Able to exist in two dimensions by appearing and disappearing at will, the Emperians are a rare and elusive race of beings scarcely seen by the outside world. Allura is the only Emperian that most sea creatures have ever had the chance to meet.

Exuberant (eg-zoo-ber-ant) – To be happy and in good health.

Feather Star – Underwater plant found close to Emperia City and shaped like a star with feather-like leaves.

Flourish (flur-ish) – To grow, thrive, or develop.

Folly (fal-lee) – A foolish action, belief, or mistake.

Genetic – Biology that deals with inherited traits that pass from parents to children.

Gran – A title of respect for the female elders of the Loch.

Gran Mama Ness – Nessandra's grandmother and the last plesiosaur to take the historic Knowledge Journey. It is through her writings that Nessandra is guided on her quest throughout the world's oceans.

Gran Morag of Morar (gran more-rag of moor-ar) – South of Loch Ness, Morag is the plesiosaur ruler of Loch Morar and guardian of the nineteen portals that lead out of the Neptune Tunnel. Only responsive to speech that rhymes, she is the one who grants permission and assistance to travelers who wish to use her portals.

Guerilla Warfare – A type of combat where small forces of irregular soldiers make surprise raids.

Healing Prism – A very special crystal located in the city of Atlantis. If a creature gets sick or injured, this crystal has the power to heal them.

Horgum – A roaming giant squid with a bad attitude, Horgum is an unwelcome visitor to the Loch and its inhabitants. He is happiest when slithering around the depths of the ocean, scaring newlings and creatures much smaller than himself.

International Council of Ocean Regulation – A fictional group of elected officials from all over the world who hear cases and pass laws that are related to conservation of the world's oceans.

Knowledge Journey – Led by a member of the Ness family, the Knowledge Journey is a search by creatures of the Loch for information and truths about the world outside their protected realm.

Kraken – The name of the family of giant squids that live in the Loch. Krakey is a member of this family and will someday, when he becomes old enough, take on the name of his father – Mon Kraken.

Lake Champlain – Located in the northwestern corner of Vermont, Lake Champlain reaches across the New York and Canadian borders. With a depth of 405 feet, the lake is thought by drywalkers to be the home of a mysterious prehistoric creature. Nessandra and her friends get to the bottom of this mystery when they meet Champ.

Light Crystals – Used to illuminate the deep waters of the Loch, the light crystals come from the far-off island of Atlantis. When new crystals are needed to replace the old ones, limericks are the only form of payment the Atlantean crystal traders accept.

Limerick – A poem of five lines in which the first, second, and fifth lines rhyme, while the third and fourth lines share a different rhyme.

Lincoln Sea – A body of water that touches the continent of Greenland on its northern shore.

Link, (the) – A psychic method of communication that only Nessandra and her family possess. Linking is physically exhausting, so Nessandra only uses this power when absolutely necessary.

Loch, (the) – Located beneath Loch Ness, the Loch is the protected home of hundreds of animal species. Most of the Loch's inhabitants prefer to stay within its boundaries. However, some creatures have been known to venture outside to try and get a peek at the strange, air-breathing creatures known as drywalkers.

Loch Ness – Located in Scotland, Loch Ness is thought by drywalkers to be about 132 meters deep – that's about 433 feet! Because of its muddy waters though, they can't be very sure where the water ends and the bottom of Loch Ness begins.

Lyrian City (leer-ee-an) – Lyrian City is where the Crystal Traders (the Shimmering Solons) trade their crystals for limericks. The Capitol of Atlantis, it is also where Atlantean citizens take refuge when the thresher sharks attack.

Mallet's Bay – A small bay connected to Lake Champlain between the towns of Winooski and Milton, Vermont.

Magical City – What the creatures of the sea call the dwelling place of the elusive Emperians. The Magical City has rarely been seen by the creatures of the ocean because, except under perfect conditions, it is invisible to the outside world.

Majestic – Grand and stately.

Mercenary – A person without loyalty or allegiance to a particular group. One who is hired to work a certain job for cash payment only. The mercenary pinnipeds that kidnap young Allura perform this task in order to receive payment from the drywalkers.

Mer Madre (mare ma-dray) – Known to drywalkers as the Atlantic Ocean.

Mer Padre (mare pa-dray) – Known to drywalkers as the Pacific Ocean.

Mid Madre Ridge – Known to drywalkers as the Mid Atlantic Ridge.

Mon – A title of respect for the male elders of the Loch.

Motley – A group of people or things consisting of a variety of different personalities or elements. Horgum calls Nessandra and her friends "a motley crew" because they are unique in their appearances and personalities.

Mrs. Cadborosaurus (cad-bore-uh-sore-us) – The proud new mother of young Caddy, Mrs. Cadborosaurus and her family are thought to live off the Pacific Northwest Coast of the United States and Canada. Known as a "Teller of Magical History," she is able to recognize an Emperian through her genetic memory. Mrs. Cadborosaurus gives Allura her first clue to discovering her past.

Narwhal (nar-wall) – A very mysterious animal, not much is known about this unicorn-like creature. They're a sly bunch though, and often swim belly up, floating motionless for several minutes–playing dead. It's not known why they do this, but this behavior gives them their name. Narwhal means "corpse whale" in Old Norse.

Neptune Tunnel – An undersea tunnel leading from the Loch to Mer Madre. Swift currents make it very dangerous, but it's the only underwater path out of the Loch.

Perpetual – A state in which a situation remains constant over time without interruption.

Pinniped (pin-a-ped) – Walruses, seals, and sea lions are all pinnipeds, but it is the walruses that kidnap young Allura. With their three-foot tusks, thick mustaches, and 2000-pound blubbery bodies, these guys seem like they would not be interested in anything but their next meal of clams, snails, and mussels.

Plesiosaur (pleez-ee-o-soar) – Roaming the oceans during the late Triassic Period (about 213 million years ago) to the Cretaceous Period, plesiosaurs are thought to have gone extinct nearly 65 million years ago. Nessandra and her parents, being members of the plesiosaur family, would beg to differ with these drywalker theories.

Prism – A solid figure whose sides are shaped like parallelograms. Crystals are most often described as prisms because of their shape.

Pyramid – A structure with a square base and four triangular sides that meet at a single point.

Renegade – A person who switches allegiance from one group to another group.

Rite of Arcking – The Rite of Arcking is a ceremony in which a young Ness breaks the surface of the water of Loch Ness for the first time. This ritual is the beginning step in the preparation toward becoming the new leader of the Loch.

Sacred (say-cred) – An object that is associated with religion.

Sargasso Sea (sar-gah-so see) – With waters that are exceptionally clear and blue, and filled with seaweed, one of the many unique things about this sea is that it has no coastline! Lying in the middle of the Atlantic Ocean, trapped between two opposite flowing currents, the Sargasso Sea slowly spins in a clockwise direction that must make all the creatures that live there dizzy!

Shimmering Solons – Residing in the Sanctuary Room in Lyrian City, these delicate but large jellyfish are the wise creatures who hold the power to grant crystals to those seeking them. Only willing to trade their crystals for limericks, the Solons understand that learning problem solving skills and acquiring knowledge are important forms of light for the mind. For creatures unwilling to develop these skills, the physical light their crystals emit will not be used to its full potential.

Species (spee-seas) – A distinct kind or group of plants or animals.

Thresher Sharks – Even though the thresher sharks attack the sunken island of Atlantis, most of them usually are not aggressive creatures. They do, however, use their long tail fins to help them corral their food since the fin can grow to be half the total length of the shark!

Tulip Tail – When Ness females fall in love, a tulip-shaped feature develops on the tip of their tails. This growth is called a Tulip Tail.

Tully Monster – Now the Illinois state fossil, about 300 million years ago the Tully Monster was once an everyday sight to see swimming near the sea bottom. And what a sight they were: transparent bodies, eyes that stuck off the side of their heads, and scissors at the end of their noses. Named after the drywalker who first discovered its fossil, Francis Tully, *Tullimonstrum gregarium* is the Tully Monster's full scientific name. *Gregarium* means "common" in Latin, but being such a strange looking creature, we think the Tully Monster is anything but common!

Western Continent – What the creatures of the sea call the North and South American continents.

White Beaked Dolphins – Found ranging from the North Atlantic Ocean on down to the Antarctic, white beaks are a friendly and curious bunch. Known for their distinctive markings, these dolphins are commonly seen in groups of ten to fifteen, but are known to congregate in groups of up to 1,500!

Wolf Eel – Normally not so grumpy as those Bolt met, wolf eels are usually shy and docile creatures. Apparently mating for life, male and female wolf eels live together in the same den for years and guard these homes relentlessly.

Zeotar (zee-o-tar) – Zeotars are ancient lightning fish that can only be found in the Loch and have rarely been seen by the outside world. With their strong tail fins and slick bodies, the legendary Zeotars are known as one of the fastest fish species and can also throw charges with incredible accuracy and distance. Bolt and his father, Mon Zeotar, are members of this fish family.